This book belongs to:

_____

_____

_____

First published 1999 by Walker Books Ltd
87 Vauxhall Walk, London SE11 5HJ

This edition published 2011

2 4 6 8 10 9 7 5 3 1

"Maisy" Audio Visual Series produced by King Rollo Films for
Universal Pictures International Visual Programming

Maisy™. Maisy is a registered trademark of Walker Books Ltd, London.

Printed in China

British Library Cataloguing in Publication Data:
a catalogue record for this book is available from the British Library

ISBN 978-1-4063-3479-1

www.walker.co.uk
www.maisyfun.co.uk

Maisy's Pool

Lucy Cousins

WALKER BOOKS
AND SUBSIDIARIES
LONDON · BOSTON · SYDNEY · AUCKLAND

Maisy and Tallulah
are feeling hot.

Maisy has an idea.
She looks in her
shed . . .

and finds the
paddling pool.
Maisy blows it up.
Puff, puff, puff!

Tallulah fills the pool with water.

Maisy and Tallulah
put on their
swimming costumes.
Ready, steady...

Oh dear, the paddling pool has a hole in it!

Maisy mends
the hole with
sticky tape.
That's better.

Then along comes Eddie in his swimming trunks ...

and sits in the pool!
Oh Eddie, there's
no room for Maisy
and Tallulah.

But Eddie gives
Maisy and Tallulah
a shower.
Now everyone is cool.

Read and enjoy the Maisy story books

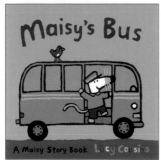

Available from all good booksellers

It's more fun with Maisy!